Disney

My Very First
Encyclopedia

with Winnie the Pooh & Friends

NATURE

Printed in Singapore
Based on the "Winnie the Pooh"
works by A. A. Milne and E. H. Shepard
ISBN Nature: 0-7868-3406-4
Visit www.disneybooks.com
Library of Congress Cataloging-in-Publication Data on file
First Edition
1 2 3 4 5 6 7 8 9 10
Written by Thea Feldman, Teresa Domnauer, Susan Ring's and Cathy Hapka
Created by Editions Play Bac, Paris, France

Hello!
Let's discover
nature!

Come with us! We're looking at nature!

You'll see all kinds of plants, from tiny seeds to giant trees.

You'll see pretty flowers, green leaves, and juicy fruits.

We'll look at the seasons together and find out about snow,
and rain, and the summer sun. We'll look up into
the sky and find out about fluffy clouds and windy days.

We'll take a look down into the ground and see what
is hidden there. We'll find out about water that rushes,
and falls, and gently flows.

Come along! Help us look at our wonderful world
of nature.

Parent's Note

This comprehensive encyclopedia about the world of nature is specially geared for the active preschool learner. Winnie the Pooh and his friends will introduce your child to the wide variety of natural wonders that exist inside and outside the Hundred-Acre Wood. Pooh and his pals will gently encourage your young discoverers to make real-life connections between the natural world in this book and themselves. The chapters of this book are organized to help young children understand how to process the wonderful world of nature that surrounds them every day.

Throughout this book, children will find their favorite characters from the Hundred-Acre Wood on hand to guide them through the various sections. Each character brings a unique voice to the world of amazing discovery that's about to unfold.

Pooh shares his sense of wonder and explorations of the world of nature throughout the book.

Tigger introduces amazing facts about some pretty Tiggerific elements of nature.

Piglet invites children to apply their newfound knowledge about nature with beautifully illustrated look–and–find pages.

Roo asks Kanga simple questions about nature, and discovers some fascinating facts.

What's inside?

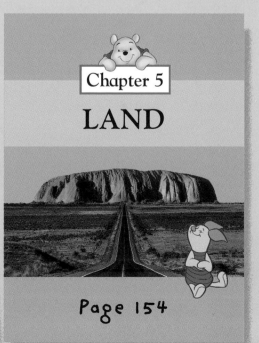

Chapter 1

SEASONS

Pooh Wonders . . .

"Are we there yet, Roo?" Pooh asked breathlessly.

Roo hopped over a log. "Almost, Pooh Bear. I think our favorite clearing is just ahead."

"Oh good," Pooh said. "Perhaps when we arrive, we can sit in the green grass and watch the honeybees buzzing around the flowers for a while."

"Here it is, Pooh!" Roo cried from just ahead. "We're here!"

Pooh followed his friend into a clearing. "Oh dear," he said in confusion. "This can't be the same place! Where is the green grass? Where are the flowers? Where are the honeybees? All I see in this clearing is snow!"

Roo laughed. "Silly Pooh," he said. "It's winter now."

"Winter?" Pooh repeated. "Why, so it is. But why should that make things look so different?"

"Everything is different in the winter than it is in the summer," Roo explained.

"My mom told me all about it. In the summer, the air is warm and the flowers bloom.

In winter, the air is cold, the flowers go away, and snow covers the grass."

Pooh blinked. "Oh I see," he said. "That must be why the view is always changing outside my windows. I always did find that rather confusing."

Roo laughed again. "If you think that's confusing, just wait until I tell you about spring and autumn!"

"C'mon, let's learn about the seasons!"

Baby birds are born in the spring.

In some places, fall brings cool, windy weather.

"Owl, what is a season?"

The seasons are different times of the year. The four seasons are called spring, summer, fall, and winter.

Each season is about three months long. In some parts of the world, the weather changes as the seasons change.

People, plants, and animals change with the seasons, too. The seasons change slowly, year after year.

We go from spring to summer to fall to winter, and back to spring again.

In some places, winter brings cold, snowy weather.

In some places, spring brings warm, sunny weather.

"Seasons are different around the World."

- When it is summer in one part of the world, it is winter in another.
- Some places have hot weather all year long.
- There are even places, likethe South Pole, where it is cold every day of the year!

Let's turn the page to read more about the seasons.

In some places, summer brings strong thunderstorms.

Snails come out after spring showers.

Discover Spring!

"Spring is the best time for picnics, isn't it, Pooh?"

"Why, yes, Piglet. But any time is the best time for honey!"

How About That!

Spring is here, and things are changing all around you. The warm sun is melting the winter snow and ice. This little stream has been quiet all winter long. Now that it's spring, the stream is filled with water and runs as fast as a river.

It's Around You!

The warm spring sun feels good after the cold of winter. As winter turns into spring, the days grow longer. Now, it stays light outside later in the evening. That means there's more time to play outside before dinner.

Spring Surprises

All winter long, the trees have rested. Now, spring brings a wonderful surprise. These tiny green buds like the warmer weather. Slowly, the little buds open up and bloom into beautiful spring flowers.

8

Brightly colored flowers blossom in the spring.

After a long winter, nature wakes up in the spring.

Lots of baby animals are born in the spring.

New green leaves grow in the spring.

Spring Weather

"It's a wet spring day, isn't it, Eeyore?"
"Very wet. Probably rain all day."

How About That!

Spring flowers are blooming all around. The flowers like the warmer weather, and they like the spring rainstorms, too. Rain  helps the flowers grow big and beautiful.

It's Around You!

Just like the flowers, animals like rainy spring days, too. After it rains, take a walk outside. You might see a little snail crawling around on the wet leaves. You might even spy an earthworm wriggling in the mud.

Weather Watch

The sun is still hiding behind the dark, gray rain clouds. But as the spring rains fall, plants are growing and baby animals are being born. The earth is getting ready for the summer season.

Spriny Happeninys

"Those baby squirrels are tiny, Pooh!"

"They're even smaller than you, Piglet."

How About That!

In the spring, many animals shed their fur. They don't need their heavy winter coats to keep them warm. Even cats and dogs lose their fur. The spring days are warmer, and animals feel cooler with less fur.

It's Around You!

These baby birds are hungry for worms. Their mommy finds lots of worms for them in the spring. The ground is soft now after being cold and hard all winter. Worms are easy to find, crawling around in the soil.

Spring Friends

Buzz, buzz! Honeybees are busy in the spring, too. They buzz from flower to flower to drink nectar. They use the sweet nectar to make honey. The bees will be busy making honey all through the spring and into the summer.

These babies squirrels will soon play outside their nest.

Discover Summer!

"It's a lazy summer day, Pooh."

"I think it's just the kind of day for a nap, Piglet."

How About That!

In the summer, the days are longer. There are places in the world where it stays light out all day and all night. In those places during summer, it's still light outside even when people go to bed!

It's Around You!

Summer is a time for growing. Bees and butterflies visit the flowers on fruit and vegetable plants. The insects help the flowers grow. Soon the little flowers will turn into beautiful summer fruits and vegetables.

More Signs of Summer

In the spring, this tree had only tiny leaves on its branches. With each sunny day, the little leaves grew and grew. Now that summer is here, the tree is covered with big green leaves.

The sun warms the ocean water in the summer.

Insects are out and about in the summer.

Summer trees are full of bright green leaves.

Sunflowers grow tall in the summer.

Summer Weather

"Why don't we cool off and go for a swim, Piglet?"

How About That!

Sometimes summer days can be too hot! This dog has found a great way to cool off. Both animals and people like to cool down in the water when it's hot outside. Pools, ponds, and lakes are fun places to swim in the heat of the summer.

It's Around You!

The hot summer weather brings mosquitoes. On summer evenings, you might notice these insects flying near you and trying to take a little bite. The buzzing sound a mosquito makes comes from its wings' flapping very, very fast!

Weather Watch

Summer days can bring clear, blue skies. Sometimes, though, there are strong thunderstorms in the summer. The storms fill the sky with dark, gray clouds. Rain pours, and thunder crashes loudly. When the storm ends, the sun will shine again.

Summer Happenings

"Hurry, Rabbit. Let's count the butterflies before they fly away."

How About That!

Even though it's hot outside, animals and insects are very active in the summer. This grasshopper lives in a meadow. It likes to leap from plant to plant. Leaves that grow nice and green in the summer are its favorite food.

It's Around You!

Even summer nights are busy times for some animals. These baby raccoons were born in the spring. Raccoons like to sleep during the day and go out at night. Now, these babies are old enough to go exploring with their mommy.

Summer Around the World

In Australia, it's summertime at Christmas. They have insects called Christmas beetles. On summer nights, they like to be near bright lights.

Hummingbirds sip nectar from flowers with their long beaks.

Looky, looky!

Summer is the time when some caterpillars do something very special. This little caterpillar was curled up in a hard shell for twelve days. Then it turned into a beautiful yellow butterfly.

Wow, that's a long way to go!

There are some butterflies that fly 2,000 miles north to a place where the weather is cool in summer. Now, that's Tiggerific!

Hallooo!

Tiggers know that if you plant daffodil bulbs in the fall, they'll bloom in the spring! You only have to plant bulbs once. Then they will bloom into flowers again the next spring!

THAT'S TIGGERIFIC!

Br-r-r!
Did you know that rain can sometimes come down as pieces of ice? These little balls of ice are called hailstones.

Can we sing along?
Tiggers know about some tiny little frogs with great big voices. These little frogs sing very loud songs at the end of winter. They're telling us that spring is here.

Discover Fall!

"Look at the pretty colors of the leaves, Rabbit."

How About That!

Fall is here, and there are many changes outdoors. Look! The green leaves on the trees are turning red, orange, and yellow. They are slowly losing their summer green color.

It's Around You!

Now that fall is here, it's getting darker earlier. There are fewer hours of daylight. In some places in the world, the last day of fall is the shortest day of the year. Then, the winter season begins.

More Signs of Fall

Now that fall is here, it's time to put away summer clothes. People start to wear sweaters, hats, and jackets in the fall. It's too cool outside to wear shorts and bathing suits anymore!

The weather starts to get cooler in the fall.

It's fun to play in leaves.

Animals gather food in the fall.

Leaves fall from the trees in autumn.

23

Fall Weather

"My it's a blustery day, Piglet!"
"Oh d-d-d-d-dear, d-d-d-dear!"

How About That!

The fall season brings cooler weather. Animals need warmer coats in the fall, just like people do. This horse's coat will grow thicker as it gets colder outside. It will keep the horse nice and warm through the fall and winter.

It's Around You!

Fall weather can be windy, too. If you go outside on a windy fall day, you'll feel the cool air blowing on your face. You'll also see the wind moving the branches and leaves in the trees. Fall is a good time to fly a kite.

Weather Watch

Do fall days seem shorter than summer days? They are. The sun goes down earlier in the fall, and the days slowly get shorter.

24

This rabbit is sitting in the grass to protect it from the cold wind.

Fall Happenings

"Look at all those pumpkins, Pooh."

"My tummy's rumbling for some pumpkin honey."

How About That!

Fall is the time when farmers harvest many fruits and vegetables. These apples were growing all summer long. Now they are ready for people to eat through the fall and winter.

It's Around You!

In some places, corn is harvested in the fall. The farmer uses a special truck called a combine to pick the corn. The combine takes the husks and the kernels off the cob. The farmer can then use the corn to feed cows or other farm animals.

Fall Ends

Now the trees are looking bare, and so are the farmer's fields. In the morning, the ground is covered with white frost. Fall has come to an end, and winter is on the way.

Getting Ready for Winter

"Pooh, are you going to save some honey for the winter?"

"Oh. I hadn't thought about that, Piglet. Do you have any I can borrow?"

How About That!

Winter is coming, and many animals are getting ready for the new season. These geese are going to fly south before the cold weather comes. They will travel to warmer places where they can find food.

It's Around You!

Though many birds fly away in the fall, some stay through the winter. This little bird is glad to have birdseed to munch on when there isn't much food around. Other animals, like deer and rabbits, look for twigs and bark from trees to eat.

Looking Ahead

This beaver will stay for the winter, too. It is gathering branches to build its winter home. It will work hard this fall to make its home safe and cozy for the long winter ahead.

This doormouse is gathering food for the upcoming winter.

Roo Wants to Know...

Why is that flower blooming in the snow?

That flower is called a snowdrop. Snowdrops are one of the first flowers to bloom in the spring. Sometimes they come out so early that there is still snow on the ground!

What do animals do when it rains?

Some small animals, like mice, hide under leaves. Bigger animals find shelter under trees. Some birds stay out in the rain. They just fluff their feathers to keep warm.

Are all baby animals born in the spring?

No, they are not. Some baby animals, like monkeys, are born at different times of the year. Mommy animals usually have their babies at the time of year when there is a lot of food around to feed them.

Why do leaves fall from the trees?

In the fall, leaves drop off the trees because they dry out. Leaves don't get as much water in the fall as they do in the spring and summer.

Why do crickets sing so loudly in the summer?

In the summer, boy crickets sing loud songs so that girl crickets can find them.

Why do birds sing so loudly in the spring?

Male birds sing loud songs in the spring so that female birds can find them. And a male bird's songs let other birds know where he and his mate are going to build their nest.

Discover Winter!

"It's so cold out, Pooh!"
"But it's nice and cozy by the fire."

How About That!

The fall days have slowly changed from cool to very cold. Winter is here. Outside, the colorful leaves of fall are gone, and the trees are bare. You might even see some sparkly frost on the grass in the morning.

It's Around You!

Now that it's winter, you'll need to bundle up when you go outside. Put on your hat, your boots, and a heavy winter coat. Don't forget your scarf and mittens!

More Signs of Winter

These little footprints in the snow were made by a red fox. It hunts through the woods and meadows, looking for food. The fox will go exploring, even on the snowiest of days.

Frost sparkles on the windows in the winter.

Animals work harder to find food in the winter.

Some countries get lots of snow in the winter.

Some trees are bare in the winter.

Winter Weather

"Piglet, these snowflakes would taste especially good with some honey!"

How About That!

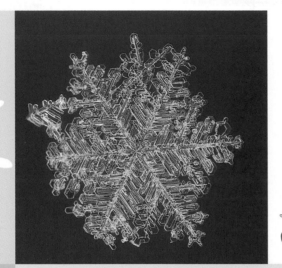

Snowflakes are made of tiny drops of water. When it's warm out, the drops of water fall as rain. In the winter, the water drops freeze and turn into tiny ice crystals that fall as snowflakes.

It's Around You!

Look at these beautiful snowflakes! They are so tiny, one can sit on your pinky. All snow is made of hundreds of thousands of these tiny snowflakes. And each one of those snowflakes is different!

Weather Watch

These trees are covered with a blanket of snow. They will rest through the winter, until spring comes and the snow melts. Then the trees will start to grow buds and little green leaves once again.

Let's Discover Winter Happenings

"I like your antlers, Eeyore."

"Didn't think you'd know it was me."

How About That!

Some animals have no trouble living in cold, snowy weather. This moose has a thick, furry coat to keep it warm. It also has wide hooves to help it walk through the snow.

It's Around You!

Back in the fall, this squirrel collected acorns and buried them. Now that it's winter, the squirrel has plenty to eat. It can smell the nuts underground, even if they're covered with snow. This makes it easy for the squirrel to find its buried snacks!

Winter Friends

This weasel has a special trick for winter. Its coat changes from brown to white. Now the weasel blends in with the snow. This helps it hide from danger. When spring comes, it will shed its white coat for a brown one again.

Winter Sleep

"Piglet, I think it's a good time for a long nap."

How About That!

When cold weather comes, some animals spend the winter sleeping. Frogs and toads burrow into the mud. They rest there all winter and hop out of the mud when spring comes.

It's Around You!

Ladybugs find cozy places in which to spend the winter. They like to snuggle up together under tree bark or under logs. You might find a ladybug in your house, looking for a warm place to sleep.

Winter Friends

During the fall, this bear ate lots and lots of food. Now it's ready to go to sleep for the winter. It will curl up inside a cave and sleep for about six months. When spring comes, the bear will wake up. And it will be hungry again!

A baby squirrel snuggles up for warmth during winter.

Is it time to wake up yet?

Tiggers know that the North Pole and the South Pole have times called light and dark seasons. That's because it stays dark outside, even during the day in winter, and it stays light outside even during the night in spring.

Hey, you! Where are your antlers?

Did you know that a daddy deer sheds his antlers in the winter? He grows a new set every spring.

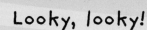

Looky, looky!

Did you know that some insects, like crickets, lay their eggs in the fall. The eggs live through the cold winter, and the baby crickets hatch in the spring!

Hey, Bigfoot!

It's Tigger here, tellin' ya that there are special shoes for walking in the snow. They're called snowshoes! Snowshoes are big and wide so they don't sink into the snow when you walk.

THAT'S TIGGERIFIC!

Snack time!

These meadow mice are getting ready for the winter. Look how they can fill up their cheeks with food! They put the food in their den and save it for later in the winter.

Look at those big ice cubes.

These houses are called igloos. And even though they're made of snow, they keep people warm.

Look and Find with Piglet!

Now you've learned about seasons, look at the picture and answer the questions below.

- What is Pooh doing?
- Where are the fox tracks?
- Where is the possum sleeping?
- What are Piglet and Roo doing?
- What is covering the trees?
- What is hanging from the tree branches?
- What has Tigger just tossed at Rabbit?

Answers

- Ice-skating
- Near the big tree behind Pooh
- In the hollow log
- Building a snowman
- Snow
- Icicles
- A snowball

43

Chapter 2

PLANTS

Pooh Wonders . . .

"Pooh!" Rabbit squawked as Pooh entered his garden. "NO! Don't step on those turnips!"

Pooh stopped. He peered at the ground, but all he could see was dirt. "Er, what turnips, Rabbit?"

"Right where you're standing!" Rabbit pointed at the dirt. "I just planted a whole row of seeds there this morning."

"Seeds?" Pooh took a step back and scratched his head. "I thought you said turnips."

"They *are* turnips!" Rabbit said. "That is, they WILL be. The seeds will grow into turnip plants, with roots and leaves. That's how plants work, you know."

"I see," Pooh said, though he wasn't sure he did. "Er, does a lettuce plant grow from a seed, too?"

"Of course," Rabbit said.

"Does a daisy grow from a seed?" Pooh asked. "Or a pine tree?"

"Yes, yes!" Rabbit said impatiently. "They all have leaves and roots, don't they? Now, stay out of the way—I have to plant my carrot seeds."

Pooh wandered off into the Hundred-Acre Wood, thinking about what Rabbit had just said. Then he noticed a tree up ahead. It had leaves. It had roots. Pooh looked up at the honey tree.

"Too bad you aren't still as small as a seed," he said hungrily. "Then I might be able to reach some honey!"

"C'mon, let's learn about plants!"

45

All plants have seeds.

"Owl, what is a plant?"

Plants grow all around us.
There are many different kinds of plants.
Trees, grass, and flowers are all plants.
Did you know that fruits and vegetables
are parts of plants? A leaf is another part
of a plant. So is a ripe, red berry.
Plants come in every different color, shape,
and size you can imagine. A plant can be
as tall as a house. It can be as tiny as your
finger.
Plants are everywhere!

Vegetables are
plants that we eat.

Insects need
plants for food.

These lemons are a fruit that grows on trees.

Wheat is a grass, which is a plant.

"Pooh, here's what makes a plant a plant!"

- All plants have roots, stems, and almost all have leaves.
- All plants make their own food from sunshine.
- All plants put oxygen back into the air.
- All plants need light, water, or air to grow.

Some plants like this tree grow very big.

47

Discover Seeds

"Go ahead, Piglet. Make a wish! Blow the seeds away!"

How About That!

What is a seed? A seed is a little package that holds a baby plant. Most plants—from tall trees to little flowers—begin their life as seeds.

It's Around You!

Seeds are found in all different kinds of fruits and vegetables. Look at the tiny seeds inside this tomato.

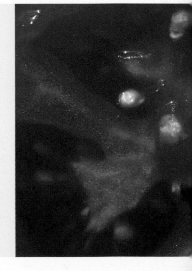

How Do Seeds Grow?

First, seeds begin in the soil. With sunshine and water, little green sprouts push their way out! Then they become big plants!

48

These seeds are tiny sesame seeds.

A coconut is the seed of a palm tree.

An acorn is the seed of an oak tree.

Dandelion seeds are light and fluffy.

49

Discover Grass

"The soft, green grass tickles my toes, Pooh."

How About That!

Grass grows in parks, gardens and on backyards. But did you know that there are more than 10,000 kinds of grass? Cereals you eat such as oats, corn, and wheat are also grasses.

It's Around You!

Some grass is very tall. It feels silky when you touch it. Other grass is short and feels prickly.

What Is Grass Used For?

Grass can be woven into baskets. It is used to make roofs on houses. Even sugar comes from a grass called sugarcane.

Wheat is a grass that is made into bread.

This grass grows in your neighborhood.

Bamboo is a grass that pandas eat.

Cattails are grasses that grow in ponds.

Discover Rice

"Rice is always nice, Piglet. Especially with just a bit of honey on it!"

How About That!

Rice is a tall, green grass. It grows in lots and lots of water. It grows in a field called a rice paddy.

It's Around You!

After some time, the rice is ready to be picked, or harvested. Then it can be made into crispy cereal. It can also be cooked until it is soft. Rice can be long, short, brown, or white.

Where Does It Grow?

Rice is grown all over the world. It grows well where it is very hot and humid. Most of the world's rice is grown in India and Asia.

This is how rice grows.

Discover Flowers

"These are for you, Eeyore. Flowers are a gift of love!"

"You'll have to love me less, then. Flowers make me sneeze!"

How About That!

Flowers are plants. You can hold a flower by its long stem. Leaves come out from the stem. And at the top, there are many colorful petals.

It's Around You!

Flowers come in all different colors. And many flowers have a wonderful sweet smell. Flowers don't last very long. But when one is finished, a new flower is ready to greet the day.

Who Loves Flowers?

People love flowers. But bees, butterflies, hummingbirds, and bats love flowers, too. They sip the sweet nectar from inside flowers. Then they fly off to find more flowers!

Roses are flowers that smell sweet.

Tulips are flowers that come in all different colors.

A bird-of-paradise flower looks like the head of a bird.

Daisies are flowers with many petals.

Discover Sunflowers

"Why are these sunflowers so tall, Pooh?"

"Why, Piglet, that makes them closer to the sun!"

How About That!

Sunflowers are the tallest flowers in the world. Some have grown to be more than 25 feet high. That's taller than a giraffe!

It's Around You!

Tiny seeds grow inside the middle of the sunflower. Many birds visit sunflowers to eat the seeds. They make a yummy snack.

Where do they grow?

Sunflowers grow all over the world. You can find them in many people's backyard gardens. They also grow in big fields.

Sunflowers turn their head toward the sun.

What's that smell?

The rafflesia is the stinkiest flower in the world. It smells like rotting meat. But flies love it. It is also the largest type of flower in the world.

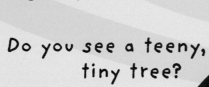

Look out! Here comes more bamboo!

Bamboo is the tallest grass in the world. And it grows fast. It can grow as much as one foot in just a single day!

Do you see a teeny, tiny tree?

This is the smallest type of tree. It is the dwarf willow. It only grows as big as your finger!

THAT'S TIGGERIFIC!

Hoo-hoo! Look at those big leaves!

The biggest leaves are from the raffia palm tree. They grow to be 65 feet long. That's as long as a tennis court.

Lots and lots of leaves!

A big oak tree can have as many as 250,000 leaves. That sure makes some good hiding places.

Fuji, Rome, and Delicious

These are just a few names for different types of apples. But there are a lot more than that. In fact, there are more than 7,000 different kinds of apples.

Discover Trees

"You know, Pooh, trees give us shelter and food."

"Thank you, trees!"

How About That!

Trees are the tallest plants. The big, middle part of a tree is the trunk. Trees also have branches that spread out from the trunk. And leaves wave to you from the ends of the branches!

It's Around You!

Since trees live outdoors, they have their own special coat to protect them. It is called bark. Bark can be smooth, rough, brown, and even white.

What Do Trees Give Us?

Trees give us so many things. We get apples, chocolate, wood, nuts, and even paper from trees. Trees also give us a fun place where we can play.

Palm trees grow where it is hot and humid.

A spruce tree has pinecones.

Redwood trees are some
of the biggest trees in the world.

Baobab trees grow so big that sometimes
people live in them!

Discover Oak Trees

"Pooh, did you know that an oak tree is a very busy place?"

How About That!

Look up, up, up! This big tree is an oak tree. Oak trees are strong, sturdy trees. Their leaves provide cool shade in the summer.

It's Around You!

Kerplunk! In the autumn you might be able to hear acorns drop to the ground. From tiny to tall . . . even the biggest, tallest oak trees begin as little acorn seeds.

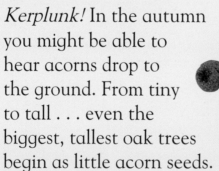

Who Lives There?

So many different creatures make oak trees their home. They crawl up, run down, dig under, and poke their heads out. What do you see in this oak tree?

Discover Vegetables

"Pooh, look at all the yummy vegetables."

"But Rabbit, I prefer honey."

How About That!

What are parts of a plant that people eat? Vegetables! Lettuce is a plant's leaves, celery is a stem, broccoli are flowers, and beets are roots.

It's Around You!

Look at all the bright colors of these vegetables: red tomatoes, purple eggplant, yellow corn, red and yellow peppers, and green zucchini.

Where Do Vegetables Grow?

Farmers grow a lot of vegetables. Other people grow vegetables right in their own backyards. You can even grow some vegetables on your windowsill!

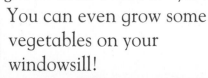

Corn is often eaten right on the cob.

Lettuce tastes good in salads.

Potatoes are eaten all around the world.

Peas come in pods.

Discover Carrots

"Let's bring some of these yummy carrots to your friends, Rabbit."

"We better hurry, Pooh! I might eat them all first!"

How About That!

A carrot is a vegetable. People eat carrots raw or cooked in soups or stews. Horses and bunnies love to eat carrots.

It's Around You!

You can't beat the crunch of a carrot! Carrots not only taste good but they are also good for your eyes. If you eat enough carrots, they can help you see better.

How Does a Carrot Grow?

We eat the orange part of the carrot. That is the long root of the plant. It grows under the ground.

Roo Wants to Know...

What do plants eat?

Most plants make their own food. But a few plants actually eat insects.

What are the little dots in a potato called?

Those little dots are called "eyes." But potatoes are vegetables so they can't really see.

How many acorns grow on an oak tree?

In one season, an oak tree can have as many as 50,000 acorns!

Why did they name that green apple after a grandma?

The Granny Smith apple is named for an elderly Australian woman named Maria Anne Smith. She was the first one to grow that type of apple.

Do people always throw away the parts of a vegetable they don't eat?

Not always. Many years ago, green carrot tops were used to decorate people's hats!

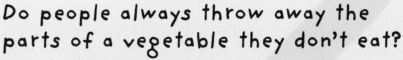

Can you tell how old a tree is?

When a tree has died, look at the trunk that is left. You can count the rings. One ring equals one year.

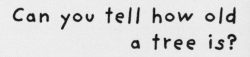

Discover Fruit

"Bananas are yummy, aren't they, Rabbit?"

"Indeed, Pooh! And they come in their own nice, neat little package!"

How About That!

A fruit is a part of a plant that holds seeds. Crispy apples, slurpy watermelons, and plump plums are all fruits.

It's Around You!

Fruits can taste sweet and mushy like bananas. They can also taste sour like lemons. What fruits do you like?

How Do Fruits Grow?

Many fruits grow on trees and bushes. But some fruits, like these strawberries, grow all along the ground.

Bananas grow in bunches.

Oranges are juicy and sweet.

Lemons taste sour.

Raspberries are red and slightly fuzzy.

71

Discover Apples

"Let's bake an apple pie, Piglet. There's nothing like a little apple pie with a lot of honey!"

How About That!

Apples are fruit that grow on apple trees. Apples can be red, green, and yellow. If you cut an apple open, you can see the little seeds.

It's Around You!

Crunch! Slurp! Snap! Those are all sounds that mean someone is biting into a juicy apple. No matter what color it is, an apple is a yummy fruit.

Who Eats Apples?

Lots of people eat apples. But that's not all! Horses, rabbits, turtles, and even birds enjoy apples, too.

Discover Leaves

"There is nothing like some big green leaves to help a bear stay cool in the summer."

How About That!

A leaf is a part of a plant. Leaves grow out from branches and stems. Leaves have a big job to do. They make food for the plant.

It's Around You!

Leaves can look like circles, hearts, triangles, fans, arrows, and needles. They can have pointed or rounded edges. Leaves can be prickly, too.

Which Plants Have Leaves?

All plants have leaves. Trees and flowers have leaves. Vegetables and fruits have leaves. Even this pine tree has sharp, pointed leaves called needles.

74

lder leaves will loose their leaves in the fall.

A palm tree has long, thin leaves.

A cactus has thick leaves to hold water.

A fern leaf is made up of many little leaves.

75

Discover Bromeliads

"Those leaves must be very good friends.
Look how close together they grow!"

How About That!

This thick leaf is from a very special plant. It is called a bromeliad. It grows only in places that are very hot and wet.

It's Around You!

You can see bromeliad leaves at your grocery store. Just look at a pineapple. Can you see the thick, green leaves? Pineapples are bromeliads.

Who Lives in Bromeliads?

Can you see what is hiding among the bromeliad leaves? It is a tiny frog. The leaves collect little pools of water. That is where the tiny frogs hide.

Some bromeliads can grow directly on tree bark.

Discover Gardens

"That is such a beautiful garden! I feel happy just looking at it."

How About That!

A garden is a place where people grow plants. A garden can have vegetables, fruits, or flowers . . . or all of these plants growing together.

It's Around You!

Every garden needs some very special things in order to grow. These tomatoes, for instance, need lots of sunshine. Their long stems, called vines, grow up toward the sun.

What Else Does a Garden Need?

A garden needs to be planted in good, healthy soil. Also, as the plants grow, they need sunshine and water. Gardens need a lot of care and attention.

This vegetable garden will produce lots of flavorful vegetables.

THAT'S TIGGERIFIC!

What is that giant?

It is a type of cactus, called the saguaro.
It is the biggest type of cactus plant. It can
grow 75 feet high. That is as high
as a seven-story building.

Now THAT'S old!

This bristle cone pine is one of the oldest trees in the world. It is about 3,000 years old. The oldest tree in the world is called Methuselah. It grows in the United States. It is almost 5,000 years old!

It's too big to get your arms around it.

The biggest tree in the world is a giant sequoia. It's named General Sherman. This tree weighs more than twenty-five cars.

No small seed.

The largest type of seed in the world is the coco-de-mer palm. It can weigh 50 pounds. That is as much as thirty coconuts!

Hey! Who names these plants, anyway?

There is a tree called the monkey ball. It has a round, green fruit that looks like an orange.

Look and Find with Piglet!

Now you've learned about plants, look at the picture and answer the questions below.

- How many heads of lettuce are in Rabbit's garden?
- What has Pooh found in the tree?
- How many carrots remain to be picked?
- What is Kanga doing?
- What does Roo have in his hand?
- How many apples are in the tree?
- What does Rabbit have in his garden to keep the birds away?

- A scarecrow
- 5
- A dandelion
- Picking raspberries
- 3
- A beehive
- 5

Answers

Chapter 3

WATER

Pooh Wonders . . .

"Hello, Eeyore," Pooh said. "What are you doing?"

Eeyore was staring into the river. "I was just wondering," he said, "why this water is always in such a hurry."

"Oh!" Pooh stood beside Eeyore.

The river raced past, never slowing. "That's a very good question, Eeyore."

Eeyore blinked. "It is?" He sighed. "I didn't think it was anything special."

"Is water always in such a hurry?" Pooh wondered. "Let's find out."

He and Eeyore wandered through the Hundred-Acre Wood until they came to a pond.

"Hmm." Eeyore stared at it. "This water isn't in any hurry."

"You're right, Eeyore," Pooh agreed.

"Only once in a while," Eeyore mumbled. "And mostly by accident."

Next they found a waterfall. The water tumbled down quickly. "There's some water that's in a BIG hurry," Pooh said. "It can't even wait to find an easier way down!"

Soon they came across a puddle. "This water isn't in any hurry at all," Eeyore said.

Pooh sat down beside the puddle to think. "Some water is in a hurry," he muttered. "Some water ISN'T in a hurry. What can it mean?"

He thought and thought—until he felt a drop on his nose.

"Oh dear," Eeyore said. "It's starting to rain."

Now Pooh and Eeyore were the ones in a hurry. They ran toward Pooh's house as the rain hurried down toward the ground, forming puddles that were in no hurry to go anywhere.

"Maybe water isn't always in a hurry, Eeyore," Pooh cried. "But it's always very WET!"

"C'mon, let's learn about water!"

85

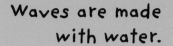
Waves are made
with water.

Rain is water that
falls from the sky.

"Owl, water, water everywhere!"

Water drips. It flows. It splashes. You can see it fall down from the sky as raindrops. You can see water in lakes and ponds. It rushes down mighty rivers, and gently flows down little streams. Water can be a powerful waterfall, or a silent, still puddle. Water fills the oceans all around the world. Every living thing needs water. People drink it, fish swim in it, whales splash in it, and birds bathe in it. Water is everywhere!

Waterfalls can be
big or small.

Icebergs are made
from frozen water.

A seal is an animal that lives in the water.

"Pooh, here's what makes water water."

- Water can be a liquid. It takes the shape of its container.
- Water can be a solid. It freezes into hard ice.
- Water can be a vapor. It goes into the air as steam, or as a cloud.

Rivers and streams flow with water.

Discover Rain

"Piglet, the rain is giving the flowers a nice shower."

"I didn't know they were dirty, Pooh.""

How About That!

What is rain? Rain is water that comes down from the sky. It begins as clouds. Soon the clouds get full. Then the rain falls down in little drops.

It's Around You

Drip, drip, drip. You can watch the rain hit the ground. You can hear it tap at your windowsill. You can see it make puddles on the sidewalk. And you can splash in it, too!

Who Needs Rain?

All living things need rain. Rain makes a cool drink for thirsty flowers. It makes a nice bath for birds. It is a gift from the clouds to the earth.

Discover Oceans

"Gee, Piglet. An ocean sure is big."
"Even bigger than an elephant's bathtub, Pooh!"

How About That!

An ocean is a big, big body of water. Many plants and animals live deep down under the ocean. Big waves roll in and out, and splash upon the seashore.

It's Around You

You can see an ocean when you go to the beach. That is where you can hear the crashing waves. You can also feel and taste the salty ocean water.

What Do Oceans Do?

The water in an ocean is always moving. This moving water is called a current. Ocean currents put heat into the air. This is how the oceans help the earth stay warm.

The Atlantic Ocean has beautiful colors.

Discover Beaches

"What's that noise, Piglet?"
"That's the sound of the ocean."

How About That!

A beach is where the ocean meets land. Most beaches are covered in soft sand. If you look carefully, you can find many gifts the ocean brings up on the beach.

It's Around You

You can find big and little shells on a beach. Each shell was once a home for a sea creature. Seaweed is a kind of plant that grows in the ocean. It often gets washed up on the sand.

What Else Is at the Beach?

A tide pool is a little rocky place at the beach. Waves splash over the rocks that are home to many living things. Starfish, crabs, snails, and little green plants can be found in tide pools.

Discover Ocean Life

"Look, Pooh! Those dolphins are jumping out of the ocean to say hello."

Many different kinds of animals live in the ocean. Giant whales, graceful dolphins, and powerful sharks live there. It is filled with fish of every color you can imagine. And they feed on all kinds of plants that grow in the ocean's waters.

The biggest creatures in the world make their homes in the ocean. They are blue whales. These whales are larger than any dinosaur that ever lived, and weigh about as much as thirty elephants!

A type of seaweed, called kelp, grows in the ocean. It grows so thick and large that it forms kelp forests in the water. Kelp is used by many sea creatures. They eat it, hide in it, and some times even sleep in it.

94

That's one big ocean!

The Pacific Ocean is the biggest ocean in the world. It almost goes all the way around the world.

Night-lights under the water?

In some oceans, tiny little plants give off light and make it glow. You could read a book by the light, it is so bright.

THAT'S
TIGGERIFIC!

It's a good thing the ocean is big!

That's where blue whales live. They can grow to be 94 feet (29 meters) long. That is bigger than any dinosaur that ever lived.

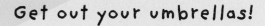

Hey! That's a lot of ice!

The biggest iceberg was larger than the whole country of Belgium. It was more than 200 miles long and 60 miles wide.

Get out your umbrellas!

In just one day, 72 inches of rain fell on one city in Africa. That much rain is as tall as a six-foot man!

What's green and brown and grows very fast?

It's seaweed. The seaweed off the coast of California is the fastest-growing plant in the world.

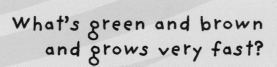

Discover Rivers and Streams

"A river looks like a fun place."
"Let's go for a boat ride."

How About That!

A river is a big, long body of water. A stream is a small, flowing body of water. The water in rivers and streams is not salty like the water in an ocean. They have what is called freshwater.

It's Around You

Rivers and streams do not flow in a straight line. They twist and turn as they flow, coming near cities and towns. You might even find a stream in your own neighborhood.

What Lives in Rivers and Streams?

Salmon are one kind of fish that begin their life in a stream. When they grow up, they swim up the mighty currents of a river. They always return home to the exact place where they were born.

The water in some rivers moves very fast.

Some plants grow in streams.

These people are swimming in a river.

A stream feels cool.

Discover Waterfalls

"I can feel the cool, refreshing mist of that waterfall all the way over here, Eeyore!"

How About That!

Woosh! Water rushes over a high cliff, pouring huge amounts of water down, down, down. That is a waterfall.

It's Around You

Waterfalls are powerful! And they make a big noise. The water dropping down over the land makes a loud, booming roar.

Where Are Waterfalls?

There are waterfalls all over the world. Many of them have names. The highest waterfall is called Angel Falls in South America. It is more than 3,000 feet high!

White Waterfalls, North Carolina, United States

Discover Lakes and Ponds

"Pooh, let's go for a swim!"

"Not until I finish with my honey, Rabbit."

How About That!

A lake is a large body of water. It is like a huge swimming pool in the earth. Some lakes are very deep. A pond is smaller than a lake, and not as deep. Lakes and ponds are filled with freshwater, just like rivers.

It's Around You

Lakes and ponds are home to many plants and animals. Bright green lily pads, with pretty flowers, grow in ponds. They are a nice place for frogs to take a rest.

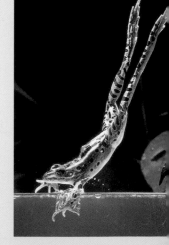

Who Else Lives in Lakes and Ponds?

Beavers live in lakes and ponds, and they love to swim. They use their sharp teeth to cut down trees. That is how they get the wood to build their homes on the water.

People enjoy fishing in a lake.

These houses have backyards right on a lake.

Ducks swim in ponds.

Some ponds freeze in the winter.

103

Discover Marshes

"Gee, do all those birds live in marshes?"

How About That!

Marshes and swamps are very special places. Swamps are found in areas that are very hot. Marshes are mostly near rivers and lakes. They are both shallow and muddy, and filled with all kinds of plants and animals.

It's Around You

You can hear bugs buzzing and bullfrogs calling. You can see birds nesting, and turtles resting, all at a marsh or a swamp!

What Else Lives in a Marsh or a Swamp?

Alligators live in both marshes and swamps. These reptiles like to swim, but they also come up on to the land. Alligators make their nests from the plants they find along the muddy banks.

A marsh is home to many birds.

People can take a boat ride through a swamp.

Mangrove swamps a near the sea.

Swamps are hot, wet, muddy places.

Roo Wants to Know...

What Is at the Bottom of the Ocean?

Deep down, the very bottom of the ocean is covered in mud. There also are tiny plants and shells. But there are some places that are too deep to know about for sure.

What is ice?

Ice is water that is very, very cold. It has gotten so cold, that it has frozen. If you make ice warm again, it will turn back into water.

Are all rivers the same?

No. Some rivers are deep. Some are shallow. Rivers can be muddy or crystal clear.

Do any animals besides seals swim in the polar waters?

Polar bears, walruses, and whales all swim in the smallest ocean on earth. It is called the Arctic Ocean, and it is at the North Pole.

Do shells grow?

Yes. Most shells grow very slowly. But they only grow while they are home to the animal they contain. Once the animal leaves, the shell stops growing.

Is there a lot of water on the Earth?

Our planet Earth is covered with more water than land. Sometimes it is called the Blue Planet. That is because of all the water.

Discover Polar Regions

"I'm glad I'm a Pooh Bear in the Hundred-Acre Wood and not a polar bear in the cold!"

How About That!

Where are the two coldest places in the world? The North Pole and the South Pole. They are both so cold that most of the water there has frozen and turned to ice.

It's Around You

What is black and white and waddles all over? A penguin! You can see thousands of penguins diving into the cold, cold water, at the South Pole.

Where are the Polar Regions?

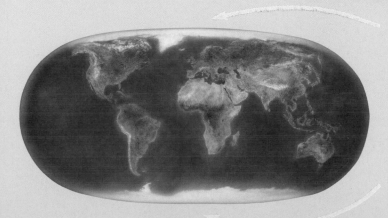

The North Pole is at the top of the earth. It is also called the Arctic Circle.

The South Pole is at the bottom part of the earth. It is also called Antarctica.

You have to keep warm in the polar regions.

People fish through a hole in the ice.

Large icebergs float in the cold polar waters.

These young Arctic foxes play in the snow.

Discover Icebergs

"Gee, Piglet, the ice is nice. But what I like most is to be warm as toast."

How About That!

A glacier is like a huge river of ice. It begins as snow on top of a mountain. Then, over thousands of years, the snow turns to ice. Big chunks of ice that break off and fall into the ocean are called icebergs.

It's Around You

Icebergs and glaciers are huge. A glacier can be hundreds of miles long. Icebergs are often as big as mountains. But icebergs are even bigger than they look. That is because more than half of an iceberg is hidden under the water.

Where are Icebergs and Glaciers?

Glaciers and icebergs are often in the polar regions where it is very cold. The countries of Newfoundland and Greenland see a lot of them. Glaciers are also found high up in mountains all around the world.

This is an iceberg. It's really big. You can only see one third of it above water.

Discover Geysers

"Piglet, look at that hot water coming out of the ground."

"That reminds me, Pooh. I would like to make a cup of tea."

How About That!

Geysers and springs are holes in the ground. But they are not ordinary holes. They have hot water coming out of them. The water gets warm deep inside the earth. A geyser is like a tea kettle. When the water gets very, very hot, it comes shooting up into the air.

It's Around You

Are these monkeys taking a bath? They are actually keeping warm. They live in northern Japan where it is very cold and snowy. So, they warm up in the natural hot springs that flow from deep inside the earth.

What is the Most Famous Geyser?

The most famous geyser is called Old Faithful. It is in the United States. Some geysers shoot out water, or erupt, every hundred years. But Old Faithful erupts just about every hour. People come from all around the world to see it.

Pohutu and Prince of Wales geysers, in Rotorua, New Zealand

113

Hey! Some lily pads are bigger than you are.

The largest lily pads are in South America. They can be as big as 5 feet across.

Well, hello there!

When seals swim under the frozen sea, they chew the ice above their heads. This makes a hole so they can pop their heads out to breathe.

Some waves are giant sized.

They are called tsunamis. A tsunami can be higher than a house and move faster than a jet. One of the biggest was 278 feet high.

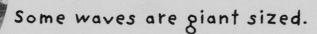

THAT'S TIGGERIFIC!

Can you touch the bottom with your toes? Not in this lake.
The world's deepest lake is Lake Baikal in Russia. It's more than a mile deep.

Br-r-r-r. I get cold just thinking about it!
The coldest temperature ever recorded on earth was at the South Pole. It was -128°F.

It's one of the natural wonders of the world.
The waterfall called Niagara Falls in New York plunges about 180 feet.

Look and Find with Piglet!

Now you've learned about water, look at the picture and answer the questions below.

- What are Eeyore and the turtle looking at?

- What is Pooh doing?

- How many baby ducks are there?

- What animal is building its house?

- How many water lilies can you find?

- What animal is Piglet about to go swimming with?

- Can you find an insect? What kind is it?

Chapter 4

SKY

Pooh Wonders . . .

"Camping out is fun, isn't it, Piglet?" Pooh said.

"I-I think so, Pooh," Piglet said. "So far it seems to have a lot to do with lying on one's back."

Pooh looked up at the sky. "Lying on one's back makes it easy to look up."

Piglet looked up, too. "P-p-pooh!" he gasped. "Look up there–is that a heffalump?"

"I don't think so, Piglet," Pooh said. "I think it's a cloud."

"Oh," Piglet said with relief. "Good. It sure looks like a heffalump, though."

"Look at that one." Pooh pointed to another cloud. "It looks like a honeypot."

Piglet smiled. "Everything looks like a honeypot to you, Pooh."

The friends watched the clouds for a while. Then they watched the sun set. The sky grew dark.

"I guess there will be nothing to look at now," Piglet said sadly.

A tiny, sparkling light appeared in the sky. Then another, and another.

"We could look at the stars," Pooh suggested. "That bunch there looks like a . . . um . . ." He was going to say "honeypot," but changed his mind. "They look like–er– like you, Piglet."

"I never knew there was so much to see up there," Piglet said.

"C'mon, let's discover the sky!"

Pooh's tummy grumbled. "I never knew that watching the sky could make me so hungry."

Clouds can be found in the sky.

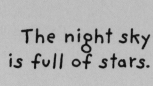
The night sky is full of stars.

"Owl, what is the sky?"

What do you see when you look up? You see the sky. The sky is above us and all around us. It surrounds the earth and gives us the air we breathe. Clouds float overhead, never keeping the same size or shape. Birds and butterflies come and go as they soar above us.

The sun fills the day with bright yellow sunshine, or turns the evening sky into shades of pink and red. The night sky is filled with silver stars and the ever-changing moon.

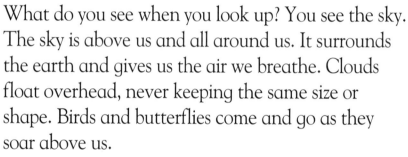
The sky is all around the earth.

The moon
comes out
every night.

"Here's what makes the sky the sky?"

- The sun is in the sky.
- The moon is in the sky.
- The daytime sky is bright.
- The nighttime sky is dark.
- The sky is always changing.

Look up! Hot-air
balloons are flying by.

Animals come out
to feed at the end
of the day.

Colors of the Sky

"Eyeore, do you want to paint a picture of the sky, too?"

"No, thank you. There are just too many colors to choose from!"

How About That!

What are the colors of the sky? Sometimes the sky is blue. Sometimes the sky is gray. In the morning, look to the east. That is where the sun rises, and the sky is filled with bright colors.

It's Around You

At the end of the day, the sun goes down in the west. That is when the sun looks like a big orange ball in the sky. A sunset also fills the sky with different shades of red, yellow, and pink.

What Are Some Other Sky Colors?

Sometimes the sky turns many shades of green and blue. This happens in places where it is very cold. These colors in the sky are called the Northern Lights.

Looking Up

"How far up does the sky go, Pooh?"
"As far as you can see, Roo."

How About That!

We get used to seeing things around us. We often look on the ground or in front of our faces. But what do you see when you look up? It is a whole different world up there.

It's Around You

Look up! What do you see? You can see birds flying by. You can see dark trees against a blue sky. You can see the sun shining through white fluffy clouds. What is looking back down at you?

How Far Up Can You See?

There is no end to the sky. You can see very far and very high. There are tools that help us see things even better. One of these tools is called a telescope. It makes things in the sky look bigger and closer.

The sky is filled with many birds.

The sky is full of colorful surprises.

Trees grow high into the sky.

Look! There is an airplane up in the sky.

Discover Planets

"Do you want to visit a planet with us, Owl?"

"We already are on a planet, Pooh.
We live on the planet Earth."

How About That!

Far, far away . . . way up in the sky . . . are big, round objects. They are called planets. There are nine planets in all. They are so far away that they are in a place called outer space.

It's Around You

Everybody you know—and don't know—lives on the same planet. We all live on planet Earth. It is the only planet we know of that has life on it now.

Can You See the Other Planets?

Sometimes you can see planets in the sky. They look like stars, shining down at night. The planets that you can see most easily are Venus and Jupiter.

Jupiter is the biggest planet.

Telescopes help us learn about planets.

The Earth is a planet, too.

Mars is one of the nine planets.

Discover Stars

"The stars are twinkling in the sky, Pooh."
"I just saw one winking at us!"

How About That!

Stars twinkle and glow in the night sky. They are really very big. But they are very far away. That is why they look so little.

It's Around You

On a dark night, you can see hundreds of stars. They make pictures in the sky, like connect-the-dots puzzles. These are called constellations.

Which Stars Do We See?

Some of the stars we see have names. One star is called Sirius. It is the brightest star in the sky.

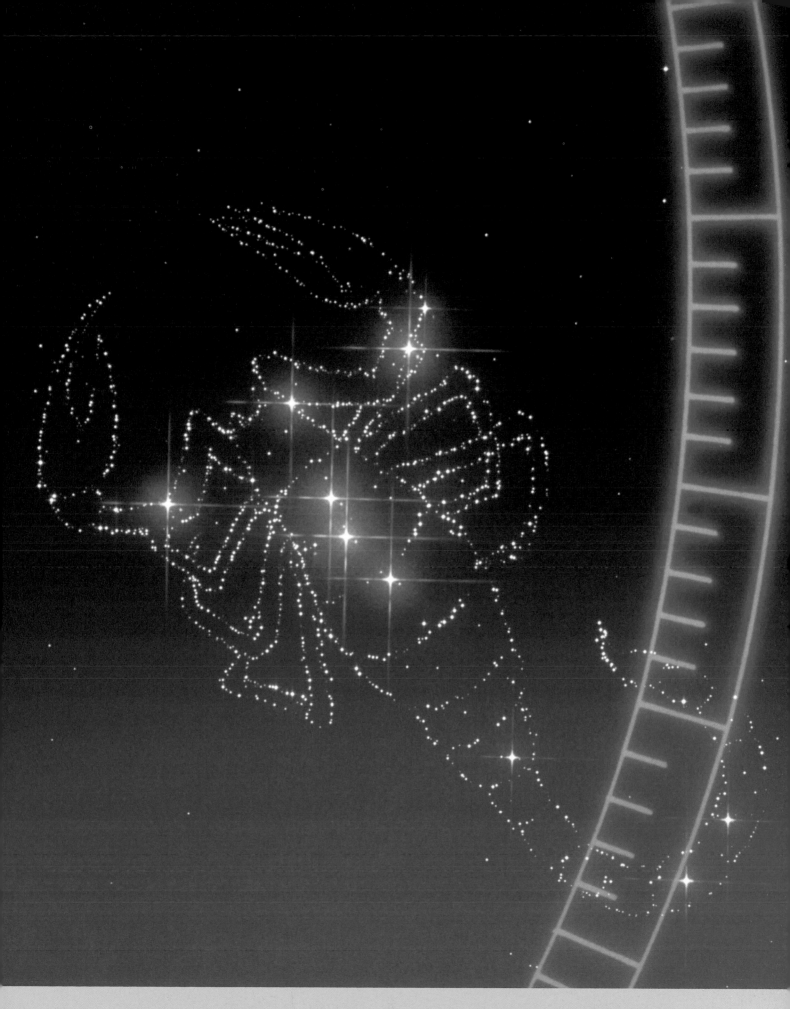

Each constellation has a special design—here is Scorpio.

THAT'S TIGGERIFIC!

Lost at sea? Just look at the sky.

Sailors have always studied the stars to help them find their way at sea.

The sun is hot, hot, hot!

The outside of the sun is 10,000° F . . . and the inside of the sun is even hotter. It is about 35 million degrees!

Hey! What time is it?

A long time ago, people did not have clocks. They could tell the time by looking at a sundial. As the day goes by, shadows move around the sundial.

Tiggers have long tails. What else has a tail?

A comet does. A comet is made of dust and ice. It speeds through outer space. Its long tail, made of dust and gases, follows close behind.

Hoo-hoo. Do you like sunny days?

The Sahara Desert in Africa is the sunniest place in the world. The sun shines there almost every day.

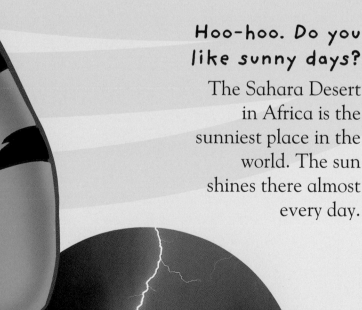

And you don't have to plug it in!

The sky has its own electricity. It is called lightning. If you see a flash of lightning in the sky, you are seeing electricity.

131

Discover the Sun

"The sunshine feels good, Piglet. Why are you sitting under that tent?"

"If I get too much sun, I will be a VERY pink piglet."

How About That!

The sun is high up in the sky. It is a big yellow ball that shines down on the earth. It is very, very far away. But the sun is so bright and hot that it warms us all.

It's Around You

The sun comes up in the morning, and it shines all day long. When the sun goes away, it is nighttime. Even though we can't see it, the sun is still in the sky at night.

Who Needs the Sun?

Every living thing needs the sun. It makes daylight. It helps to keep animals warm. Sunshine helps flowers and trees grow. People need the sun to grow, too!

Discover Day

"Gee, Rabbit. There is so much happening in the sky. It is like having our own sky show."

How About That!

Wake up! The sun has risen! It is morning. When the sun rises, it brings a new day. It will be daytime for many hours. There are many things to do during the day.

It's Around You

Daytime is a time to be up and about. It is a time to play or go to school. You might take walks, ride bikes, or skate during the day. Many animals are out during the day, too.

What Else Happens During the Day?

Sounds fill the air during the day. Dogs bark and bees buzz. You can also hear birds whistle and sing. They call to one another through the trees.

Discover the Moon

"Look, Pooh! There is a big banana in the sky." said Piglet.

"That would be so yummy with some honey on it!" Pooh said.

How About That!

The moon shines up in the sky. It is very far away, but not as far away as the sun. Sometimes the moon is very, very bright. The moon gives light to the dark night.

It's Around You

Sometimes the moon looks like a big, round ball. Other times you can only see half the moon. The moon never stays the same. It changes little by little, and goes through a cycle. Then it begins all over again.

Where is the Moon During the Day?

During the day, the moon is still in the sky. It does not go away. It is just easier to see the bright moon at night, when the sky is dark.

This is the moon close up. Its surface is covered with craters.

Discover Night

"Nighttime is so dark and a little scary, Pooh."
"I wish we had a flashlight."

How About That!

When the sun sets, the sky gets dark. Night has come. The moon shines in the sky. It is a time to slow down. It is a time when many people and animals go to sleep. This monkey is fast asleep for the night.

It's Around You

What are the sounds of the night? Sometimes you can hear insects making noise. Crickets chirp at night. They can be very loud.

What Else Happens During the Night?

Some animals are up all night long. They might fly and visit flowers that bloom only at night. Others are looking for food to eat. They sleep when daytime comes.

139

Roo Wants to Know...

Is there a man on the moon?

No. There are mountains and valleys on the moon. They make shadows that sometimes look like the moon has a face.

Can I make a rainbow?

You can't make a real rainbow. But you can see the colors of a rainbow through a prism. A prism is made out of glass. When light shines through it, it shows all of the colors in a rainbow.

Why do geese fly in the shape of a V?

The *V* shape helps the geese glide on the air currents. They don't have to work as hard. And they take turns being up front.

Do clouds have names?

There are names for the different kinds of clouds. Soft, wispy clouds are called cirrus clouds. The big, puffy ones are cumulus clouds. Dark rain clouds are called nimbus clouds.

Where are the stars during the day?

The stars are still in the sky during the day. The sun shines so brightly that you cannot see the stars. It is easier to see them against a dark sky.

What is at the end of the rainbow?

People sometimes say that there is a pot of gold at the end of a rainbow. But that is not true. You cannot reach the end of a rainbow. It can only be seen in the sky from far away.

Discover the Wind

"Tigger, hold on!"

"Don't worry, Pooh. This is way more fun than bouncing!"

How About That!

You can't see the wind. But you can feel it. It can feel very strong and powerful. It can also be a soft, gentle breeze.

It's Around You

Hold on to your hat! The wind is blowing. Sometimes the wind blows so strong that it makes a howling noise.

What Does the Wind Do?

The wind carries little seeds from one place to another. Wherever the seeds land, they have a chance to grow into new plants. So, the flowers in your backyard may have been blown there from miles away.

Discover Clouds

"Eeyore, I can see all kinds of animal shapes in those clouds!"

"I see a cloudy day."

How About That!

Clouds are fluffy and white. The wind blows them across the sky. But new clouds keep coming by. Clouds look like they are made from cotton. But they are really made of water.

It's Around You

Have you every looked up at clouds in the sky? Clouds tell us something about the weather. Dark, gray clouds tell us that it is going to rain. Fluffy clouds tell us that it will be a nice day.

Do Clouds Ever Come Close to Us?

Sometimes a cloud comes very close to the ground. So, you don't even have to look up to see it. When a cloud is close to us, it is called fog. Fog is wet and misty. It is hard to see through fog.

Discover Rainbows

"Hurry up, Pooh. I want to catch the rainbow."

How About That!

A rainbow looks like a bridge in the sky. It is made up of many different colored stripes. You can never touch a rainbow, for it is just colors in the sky.

It's Around You

If you were to paint a rainbow, what colors would you use? Rainbows have so many. Some of the colors are red, yellow, blue, and green.

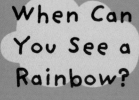

When Can You See a Rainbow?

You can see a rainbow after the rain has stopped, and the sun comes out. Sometimes you can see a rainbow over a waterfall, too.

Discover Shadows

"Owl, why is that shadow following me?"

"Because it is YOUR shadow, Pooh. That's its job!"

How About That!

When the sun shines, it makes shadows. A shadow just shows the shape of something. It can be the shape of anything.

It's Around You

Have you ever seen your own shadow? Next time you see your shadow, watch it move when you move. Your shadow will follow you everywhere.

Who Uses Shadows?

This tree is making a shadow on the ground. This shadow is a nice shady spot for lions. You feel cool when you lie in a shadow.

148

Can you guess what game this boy is playing by looking at his shadow?

How fast can the wind blow?

Port Martin, Antarctica, is the windiest place on the Earth. For one month it had winds blowing about 65 miles per hour. That's as fast as a speeding car!

That's a lot of moons!

Our planet Earth has one moon. But the planet called Saturn has 30 moons!

My, oh, my! What big eyes you have.

Many animals that are active at night have very big eyes. This helps them see well in the dark.

THAT'S TIGGERIFIC!

Flying free and easy

Did you know that some birds hardly ever flap their wings? The warm air in the sky pushes them along as they glide.

I hear that a storm's a-coming!

Every once in a while you might see a storm. The rain or snow comes down hard and fast. But did you know that there are more than 40,000 storms around the earth every single day?

Hey! Tiggers are strong. So are hurricanes.

When a very strong wind is mixed with heavy rains, it forms a hurricane. These stormy winds can knock down buildings and trees. A hurricane wind can blow as fast as 250 mph. That's as fast as an airplane!

Look and Find with Piglet!

Now you've learned about the sky, look at the picture and answer the questions below.

- Find the cloud that looks like Eeyore.
- How many birds can you find?
- What animal is sleeping in the sun?
- How many colors are there in the rainbow?
- What is Tigger looking at?
- How many insects can you find?
- Where is it raining?

Answers

- Just above the rainbow
- 6
- A lizard
- 7
- His shadow
- 3
- On Eeyore

153

Chapter 5

LAND

Pooh Wonders . . .

"No honey up there," Pooh mumbled as he stared up at a tree. "But what pretty leaves."

He walked on to another tree. He looked up. "No honey up there, either," he said. "But that bird is such a nice shade of blue. . . ."

"What are you doing up there, sonny?" a familiar voice said. Pooh looked down–and down some more. Finally, he looked all the way down into a hole in the ground. His friend Gopher was standing in the hole. "Hello down there, Gopher," Pooh said. "I was just looking up."

Gopher scowled. "Up? Up?" he cried. "Everybody wants to look up! Why doesn't anyone ever look DOWN for a change?"

Pooh shrugged. "Looking UP means seeing trees and sky and birds and all sorts of interesting things. But the only thing to see when one looks DOWN is the ground."

"Typical," Gopher grumbled. "Come with me, Pooh. I'll show you what you can see when you look down."

Pooh followed Gopher. He saw a mud puddle and a rocky gully. He saw a pile of dirt and the sandy spot at the edge of the river. He saw hills and meadows and caves. By the time he had finished, Pooh was exhausted.

"Looking down is more interesting than I thought," he told Gopher. "And I just remembered one more very nice thing about the ground."

"What's that, Pooh?" Gopher asked.

Pooh sat down. "It's so very nice to rest upon!"

"C'mon, let's discover land!"

Land can be covered
with tall mountains.

Soil from the land
can be used to
build houses.

"Owl, what is land?"

Land is all around us. It can be as big as a mountain or as small as your own backyard. It can be a grassy meadow or a dry desert. But all land is made of the same things: rocks, sand, and soil. Just look around outside!

Land can be a cozy
underground home.

156

Land can be wide and open, like a meadow.

"Pooh, here are ways we use the land!"

- People and animals use land to build homes.
- Farmers grow fruits and vegetables on the land.
- Land is full of beautiful places to see and explore.

Land can be dry and sandy, like a desert.

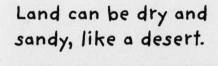

Land is where some plants can grow.

Discover Rocks

"P-p-pooh! Look at the size of that rock!"

"Piglet, I think that's the biggest rock I've ever seen."

How About That!

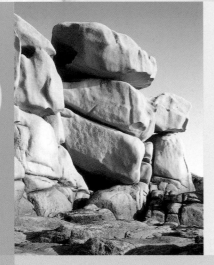

Rocks are part of the land. They are made of minerals, which are found under the ground. Minerals are made of different things, such as crystals or metals. When groups of minerals get pressed together, they become rocks.

It's Around You!

Rocks can be found all over the world. They come in many shapes, sizes, and colors. Some rocks feel smooth. Others are rough. Some rocks even sparkle!

Using the Land

This beautiful castle is made out of blocks of stone. People use rocks to build walls, houses, and many other kinds of buildings. Rock is a good thing to build with because it is heavy and strong.

158

The Etretat Cliffs, in France, are made of *solid white chalk.*

159

Discover Sand

"Sand is very good for building castles, Pooh."
"Yes, Piglet. And it's good for wiggling your toes in, too."

How About That!

Just like rocks, sand is a part of the land. Sand is made of the tiniest bits of broken rocks. You can find sand on beaches and in the desert. Sand also hides at the bottom of lakes, rivers, and oceans!

It's Around You!

Ahhh! Doesn't the sand feel good in your hands? Sand gives us a soft place to sit on at the beach. It also keeps the ocean from flooding the land.

Using the Land

Did you know that one kind of sand is used to make glass? It is heated until it is so hot that is melts. Then it is shaped into glass. Look around your house. You will see many things made from glass.

This beach has lots of sand.

Discover Soil

"What are we planting, Piglet?"

"We're planting haycorn trees, Pooh. This is the perfect place to grow haycorns."

How About That!

Do you know what soil is? It's dirt! Soil is another important part of land. It's made of tiny bits of rocks and plants. There are many kinds of soil around the world.

It's Around You!

Without soil, this little plant couldn't grow. The soil keeps the plant's tiny roots safe. And it helps the plant to stand up tall and strong. The soil also gives the plant food and water.

Using the Land

Clay is a special kind of soil. People use clay to make pottery. After the soft clay is shaped, it is baked in a very hot oven. Then it becomes strong and hard just like the plates and cups in your house!

This tractor prepares the soil for planting.

Discover Soil for Homes

"Eeyore, it looks as though your house fell down again."

"Maybe I'll make my house out of mud next time, Pooh."

Did you know that mud can be used to make homes? Some birds use mud to build their nests. Mud is made of wet soil. It helps hold twigs and straw together, just like glue.

Look! Can you see how tall these termite homes are? These termites can build mounds in the soil that are up to 20 feet tall. That's almost as tall as a house!

Soil can also be used to make bricks. Some bricks are made of clay. Others are made of mud and grass. Since mud, clay, and grass are easy to find, people have made brick homes for thousands of years.

In some places people build houses from mud.

Want to paint?

People used to make paint from rocks! They would crush up colorful rocks and mix them with water. Isn't that just Tiggerific?

Hey, bigfoot!!

Camels have special feet that help them walk in the sand. Their wide feet keep them from sinking in the sand!

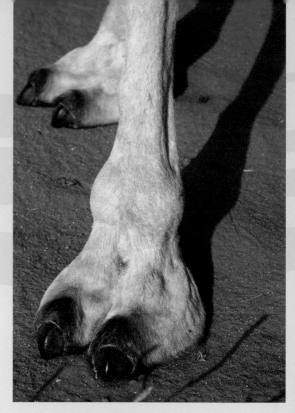

Hanging around?

Did you know that people climb in caves? These people have a funny name: spelunkers! They use special boots, ropes, and hooks to help them climb.

What's for dessert?

Guess what? There are rocks called pudding stones! They're made when different rocks and pebbles get stuck together. You might find some near oceans or rivers.

THAT'S TIGGERIFIC!

You call that clean?

Some animals like to take baths in mud! The mud helps them stay cool and keeps the bugs away.

Don't forget to take water!

This is the world's largest desert. It's called the Sahara Desert, and it's in Africa. It's thousands of miles wide!

Discover Underground Animals

"Hello, Gopher! How's life underground?"

"S-s-swell, Pooh!"

How About That!

Many animals make their homes in the soil. This mole spends most of its life underground. Moles dig long tunnels with their big, wide front claws. Moles find lots of yummy bugs and worms to eat in the ground.

It's Around You!

Have you ever seen a bird dig a hole? Kingfishers are birds that make their nests in the ground. They use their long beaks to dig. They make tunnels and nest holes in the dirt along rivers or streams.

Using the Land

Some ants make their nests underground. These tiny bugs can dig deep into the soil. The busy ants dig out long tunnels and lots of little rooms. They even make special rooms for the baby ants!

This prairie dog digs tunnels under the ground.

Discover Underground Treasures

"What are you doing, Roo?"
"I'm digging for buried treasure!"

How About That!

Did you know that gold is found under the ground? Gold is a very soft metal. After it is dug out of the ground, it is melted. Then it can be shaped into beautiful jewelry.

It's Around You!

Can you see all those sparkly crystals? The outside of this rock looks plain and gray, but the inside holds a wonderful surprise. These underground treasures are called "thunder eggs."

Using the Land

A mine is a hole dug into the earth. Miners work hard to get iron, steel, and other important metals from the ground. These metals are used to make things like cars, airplanes, boats, and even toys!

This is a quartz crystal. It comes in many different colors.

Discover Caves

"Why, what's this, Piglet?"

"P-p-pooh! It's very dark in there. I think it must be a woozle cave!"

How About That!

Look here! This is a cave. Caves are really just holes in the ground. They can be very, very deep. Some caves even have waterfalls and lakes inside of them.

It's Around You!

Have you ever seen the inside of a cave? It looks like there are icicles hanging from the ceiling and growing up from the floor. These icicles are not made of ice at all. They are made of stone.

Using the Land

Bats and other animals use caves for their homes. A cave is a safe place where they can sleep. Long ago, people used to live in caves, too!

This is the view from inside a cave.

Discover Mountains

"My, those hills are very big, Owl!"

How About That!

Mountains are part of the land that stands big and tall. They are made of different kinds of soil and rock. Mountains can be found all over the world. There are even some mountains at the bottom of the ocean!

It's Around You!

Mountains are home to many animals. Wild goats climb the rocks. Mountain lions hunt for animals. Eagles soar over the mountaintops.

Using the Land

Mountains can be fun places in which to explore. Some people like to climb up mountains. Others like to ski down them. Have you ever been to the mountains?

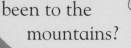

174

This is a mountain lion.

Discover Forests

"Rabbit, aren't the trees lovely?"

"Yes, they are, Pooh. It's lovely to be in the forest with you."

How About That!

Land that is covered with many trees is called a forest. There are many kinds of forests around the world. A forest is filled with plants and animals.

It's Around You!

Some kinds of forests grow in very cold parts of the world. Most of the trees that grow in these forests are pine or fir trees. Animals such as moose, caribou, foxes, and wolves live in these evergreen forests.

Using the Land

People use wood from forests to build houses and furniture, and to make paper and many other things. Whenever we cut down trees, we try to plant more of them. That way, we'll always have forests!

Roo
Wants to
KnoW...

Are bats the only animals that live in caves?

No, but there are very few animals that can live in caves. Barn owls can live in caves, along with some types of moths, butterflies, fish, and snakes.

Which is the tallest mountain?

The tallest mountain in the world is Mount Everest. It's so tall that it pokes through the clouds. Brave people who like adventures try to climb this mountain. Some people have even made it to the top.

Are deserts always hot?

No. Some deserts, like the Gobi Desert, are called "cold" deserts. The weather is very cold there. It can even snow a little bit in cold deserts!

Do some animals live under the sand?

Yes, they do. Crabs and clams tunnel into the sand to look for food. When the sea washes the sand away, they just dig down deeper.

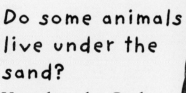

Do people live in the rain forest?

Yes, some people do live in the rain forest. They have lived there for hundreds of years, and they can teach us many things about these amazing forests.

What kinds of flowers grow in a meadow?

Dandelions, daisies, red clover, and many other kinds of flowers grow in a meadow. Meadow flowers are full of nectar for insects to eat.

Discover the Rain Forests

"Piglet, I think the Hundred-Acre Wood has turned into a rain forest."

"It certainly feels that way, Pooh!"

How About That!

A rain forest is another kind of forest. Rain forests can get as much as 160 inches of rain each year. They are usually found in parts of the world where the weather is very warm. Many kinds of plants and animals make the rain forest their home.

It's Around You!

If you like to climb trees, then you'd have a lot of friends in the rain forest. Many rain forest animals, like this spider monkey, live in the treetops. Spider monkeys have long arms and legs to help them climb through the trees. They even use their tails to hold on to branches!

Using the Land

Rain forests give us many important things. People like to eat delicious tropical fruits and nuts that grow in the rain forest. We also use special plants from the rain forest to make medicines that help people who are sick.

A rain forest in Indonesia

Discover Meadows

"Pooh, I like to play hide-and-seek in the meadow."

"I do, too, Piglet. But where is Roo?"

How About That!

A meadow is land that is wide and open and covered with grass. Many insects, plants, and animals make their homes in the meadow. Mice and bunnies hide in the tall grass. Hummingbirds and butterflies fly happily around the flowers.

It's Around You!

This woodchuck lives in a burrow in the meadow. When it feels hungry, it comes up out of its den. It looks around the meadow to make sure there is no danger near. Then the woodchuck looks around for meadow plants to munch on.

Using the Land

Some farmers grow hay in open meadows. The farmers bundle the hay in bales. Then, they use the hay to feed their cows, sheep, and other animals.

This is a meadow filled with flowers.

Discover Deserts

"Looky, looky, Pooh Boy! I found a new kind of forest!"

"Tigger, that isn't a forest. It's a desert!"

How About That!

Deserts are parts of the land that get very little rain. Most deserts are very dry and are covered with sand. Even though there is little water here, there are plants and animals that can live in the desert.

It's Around You!

Cactuses can store water inside their trunks. This helps them stay alive in the hot, dry land of the desert. A cactus feels very prickly to the touch. This keeps hungry animals from eating the cactus as a snack!

Using the Land

Some people who live in the desert use the land to raise animals. They have herds of camels, goats, and sheep. They travel through the desert to find water and places where their animals can feed.

This is the Sahara Desert.

THAT'S TIGGERIFIC!

What's yellow and black? A tigger?

Did you know that sand comes in different colors? There's white sand, red sand, black sand, and even green sand! And that's just Tiggerific!

Ah, one, two, three, four, five . . .

Rain forests can have 100 different kinds of trees! They have more kinds of trees than any other forest in the world!

Is it a mountain? No, it's a rock!

Ayers Rock is the largest rock in the world. It's located in the northern territory of Australia. It's more than 1,100 feet high and more than five miles around.

Did you know that rocks change shape?

It takes a long time, but water and wind can make rocks into different shapes!

Want a shovel?

Gophers use their front teeth to dig, along with their claws! And gophers use their tails to feel their way around tunnels!

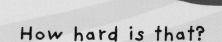

How hard is that?

Did you know that diamonds are the hardest stone in the world? If you want to cut a diamond in half, you need to use another diamond to do it!

Look and Find with Piglet!

Now you've learned about land, look at the picture and answer the questions below.

- What is Rabbit doing?
- How many bats are in the cave?
- Who is Eeyore talking to?
- Can you find a diamond?
- How many ants can you find?
- What animal is asleep in its burrow?
- Who is holding rocks in his hand?

189

INDEX

Cover photos credits from left to right:

Bios/Ruoso Hoaqui/Baccega Bios/OSF/Tyrell Hoaqui/Zefa Jacana/Cordier Jacana/Arndt Bios/Rotman Bios/Klein-Hubert Bios/von Schmieder Sunset/Holt Studio Bios/meul/Fotonatura
Title Page/copyright/introduction: Bios/Martin P 3: Hoaqui/Baccega Hoaqui/Zefa Jacana/Cordier Bios/Klein-Hubert Getty/Taxi/Du Feu

Chapter Seasons:

P.6: Getty/Image Bank/Rakke, Colibri/Smellinckx, Getty/Stone P.7: Hoaqui/Leroux, Bios/Bringard, Bios/Cancalosi, Jacana/Thomas P.8: a) Bios/Bringard b) Sunset/Zéphyr images
c) Graphic Obsession/DR P.9: ul) Sunset/Bringard ur) Getty/Taxi bl) Sunset/Wilmhurst br) Getty/Busselle P.10: a) Bios/Bringard b) Jacana/Thomas c) Jacana/Anup Shah
P.11: Sunset/F.Stock. P.12: a) Bios/Klein-Hubert b) Colibri/Smellinckx c) Bios/Fatras P.13: Sunset/Visage P.14: a) Hoaqui/Leroux b) Getty/Foodpix/Triolo/Burker c) Sunset /Brousse
P.15: ul) Sunset/World Pictures ur) Sunset/Bringard bl) Sunset/Claudie br) Sunset/Japack P.16: a) Bios/Ausloos b) Getty/Taxi c) Bios/Weimann P.17: Getty/Taxi
P.18: a) Bios/Meul/Fotonatura b) Sunset/Lacz c) Sunset/NHPA P.19: Sunset/Mc Donald P.20: caterpillar: a) Bios/Heuclin b) Bios/Ezeff c) Bios/Bringard d) Bios/Bertani left) Getty
images d) Jacana/Hofer bl Jacana/Gurawich P.21: Getty/Stone/Horgan, Sunset/Animals Animals P.22: a) Bios/Sira/GPL Bios/Bringard b) Jacana/Zefa/Marks c) Sunset/Comté
P.23: ul) Bios/Bruemmer ur) Getty/Taxi bl) Sunset/NHPA br) Bios/Delfino P.24: a) Getty/Stone b) Hoaqui/Zefa/Benser c) Getty/Stone P.25: Jacana/Dupont. P.26: a) Getty/Taxi
b) Jacana/Dulhoste c) Jacana/Schunk P.27: Getty/Stone. P.28: Getty/Taxi Bios/Klein-Hubert P.29: Bios/Gunther Jacana/Becker Jacana/Nardin Bios/Heuclin P.30: a) Sunset/Warden
b) Sunset/F.Stock c) Jacana/Walker P.31: Jacana/Danegger P.32: a) Bios/Didillon b) Getty/Stone c) Bios/Klein-Hubert P.33: ul) Hoaqui/Zefa ur) Jacana/Danegger bl) Getty/Image
Bank br) Hoaqui/Zefa/Kehrer P.34: a) Sunset/FLPA b) Getty/Stone c) Hoaqui/Detalle P.35: Hoaqui/Hagenmüller P.36: a) Sunset/Levin b) Bios/Etienne c) Jacana/Walker
P.37: Jacana/Danegger P.38: a) Sunset/Schiell b) Jacana/Schwind c) Bios/Klein-Hubert P.39: Bios/Odeur/Wildlife P.40: Bios/Ziegler Getty/Taxi Jacana/Varin Sunset/Alaska Stock
P.41: Getty/Image Bank Getty/Stone.

Chapter Plants:

P 58: a)Bios/Seitre b) Sunset/West Stock c) Sunset/Horizon Vision P 59: a) Bios/Fève b) Hoaqui/Zefa Sunset c) Bios/Noto-CamPanella d) Sunset/Reinhard
P.46: Getty/Cummins, Bios/Klein-Hubert, Getty/Foodpix, Jacana/Moiton P.47: Bios/Panais, Sunset/Marge. P.48: a) Bios/Douillet b) Jacana/Hoaqui/Bisu c) Sunset /Bringard
P.49: ul) Getty/Simon ur) Bios/Brown bl) Bios/Rosenthal br) Getty/Cummins P.50: a) Getty/Oberle b) Bios/Laurier c) Getty/Stone, Getty/Layma P.51: ul) Bios/Panais ur) Sunset/Rossi
bl) Bios/Schultz br) Getty/Christensen P.52: a) Hoaqui/Martel b) Sunset/Japack c) Bios/Le Morcy P.53: Sunset/Picturesque P.54: Getty/Davies&Starr b) Bios/Alcalay c) Jacana/Moiton
P.55: ul) GrandeurNature/Grive ur) Bios/Grospas bl) Grandeur Nature/Brioux br) Grandeur Nature/Thiriet P.56: a) Getty/Cummins b) Bios/Klein-Hubert c) Grandeur Nature/Thiriet
P.57: Grandeur Nature/Karel P.58: Getty/Taxi, Bios/Compost, Getty/Stone P.59: Bios/Halleux, Bios/Klein-Hubert, Getty/Image Bank P.60: a) Bios/Okapia/Reinhard b) Jacana/Hofer
c) Getty/Buss P.61: ul) Bios/Martin ur) Jacana/Lacoste bl) Bios/Mutzig br) Jacana/Maza P.62: a) Grandeur Nature/Aubriac b) Bios/Coll.Leber c) Jacana/Visage/Varin.
P.63:Sunset/Marge. p.64: a) Bios/Laurier b) Getty/Foodpix c) Bios/Douillet. P.65: ul) Bios/Lopez ur) Bios/Bringard bl) Bios/Chipot br) Jacana/Félix. P.66: a) Cogis/Rocher
b) Getty/Botterell c) Bios/Bringard P.67: Grandeur Nature/Aubriac P.68: Bios/Martin Bios/Gunther P.69: Getty/Image Bank, Jacana/Félix, Getty/Foodpix, Bios/Heuclin
P.70: a) Bios/Gunther b) Getty/Foodpix c) Bios/Laurier P.71: ul) Sunset/Japack ur) Bios/Klein-Hubert bl) Sunset/Canigher br) Getty/Image Bank/Mascardi P.72: a) Bios/Gunther
b) Hoaqui/Explorer/Balzak c) Jacana/Cordier P.73: Bios/Lenain P.74: a) Sunset/Holt Studio b) Bios/Gunther, Bios/Douillet c) Sunset/Gapençais P.75: ul) Jacana/Berthoule
ur) Sunset/Roger bl) Sunset/Prix br) Grandeur Nature/Brioux P.76: a) Bios/Seitre b) Sunset/Horizon Vision c) Jacana/Konig P.77: Jacana/Roguenant P.78: a) Sunset/Cavagnaro
b) Bios/Coll.Leber c) Grandeur Nature/Karel, P.Grandeur Nature/Brioux P.80: Getty/Taxi, Bios/Alcalay P.81: Sunset/NHPA, Sunset/Leeson, Bios/Martin, Bios/Van den Berg.

Chapter Water:

P.86: Bios/Rapillard, Bios/OSF/Winer, Sunset/Warden P.87: Jacana/Krasemann, Jacana/Cauchoix, Bios/Bretagnolle P.88: a) Sunset/STF b) Getty/Taxi c) Sunset/Thielemann
P.89: Bios/Rapillard. P.90: a) Bios/OSF/Winer b) Sunset/Audet c) Sunset/Picturesque P.91: Bios/Laurier P.92: a) Jacana/Tovy b) Hoaqui/PBY c) Bios/Alcalay
P.93: Sunset/F.Stock P.94: a) Jacana/Wu b) Hoaqui/PBY c) Sunset/Animals Animals P.95: Bios/Klein-Hubert P.96: Getty/Stone Bios/Foott/Panda P.97: Jacana/Wisniewski,
Bios/Cawardine, Sunset Bios/Migeon P.98: a) Bios/Gilson b) Hoaqui/Guittard c) Jacana/Cordier P.99: ul) Jacana/Cauchoix ur) Sunset/Delfino bl) Sunset/Delfino
br) Sunset/Mach 2 Stock P.100: a) Sunset/Warden b) Sunset/Delfino c) Sunset/NHPA P.101: Sunset/Picturesque P.102: a) Sunset/Photobank USA b) Bios/OSF/Dalton
c) Jacana/Leeson/PHR P.103: ul) Hoaqui/Guittard ur) Sunset/FirstLight bl) Bios/Ruoso br) Jacana/Hoang Cong P.104: a) Hoaqui/Grandadam b) Sunset/HorizonVision
c) Jacana/Polking P.105: ul) Getty/Stone ur) Getty/Taxi bl) Jacana/Lobivia br) Getty/Taxi/Downer P.106: Jacana/Wu, Bios/Bringard, Hoaqui/PBY P.107: Jacana/Freund
Bios/coll.Leber (2) Hoaqui/PBY P.108: a) Bios/Kobeh b) Bios/Sylvestre c) Getty/Taxi P.109: ul) Sunset/Alaska Stock ur) Getty/Stone bl) Sunset/Alaska Stock br) Bios/Weimann
P.110: a) Jacana/Pott b) Bios/Bretagnolle c) Hoaqui/Explorer/Monteath P.111: Sunset/Pott P.112: a) Jacana/Brehm b) Jacana/Orion Press c) Jacana/Waltz. P.113:Getty/Stone/Lamb
P.114 : Jacana/Krasemann Hoaqui/Explorer/Ducandas, Bios/OSF/Winer P.115: Sunset/World Pictures, Jacana/Wild, Sunset/World Pictures

Chapter Sky:

P.120: Sunset/Weststock Getty/Taxi Hoaqui/PBY P.121: Bios/Ruoso Getty/Stone Bios/Ruoso P.122: a) Getty/Taxi b) Jacana/Hodalic c) Jacana/Walker P.123:Jacana/Simanor
P.124: a) Hoaqui/Perousse b) Jacana/Zvardon c) Getty/Stone P.125: ul) Bios/Meilhac ur) Hoaqui/PBY bl) Hoaqui/Zefa/Freytag br) Hoaqui/PBY P.126 : a) Getty/Taxi
b) Getty/Image Bank c) Jacana/Lotscher P.127: ul) Hoaqui/Galaxy Contact ur) Getty/Taxi/Lefkowitz bl) Getty/Stone br) Getty/Stone P.128: a) Getty/Taxi b) Bios/Leduc
c) Getty/TIB/O'Hara P.129: Getty/TIB/Reginato P.130:Hoaqui/PBY, Sunset/NHPA. P.131: Hoaqui/Roy, Getty/Image Bank, Hoaqui/PBY, Hoaqui/PHR/Explorer
P.132: a) Sunset/Moulu b) Getty/Stone c) Sunset/Ant. P.133: Getty/Taxi/ISP P.134 : a) Bios/Alcalay b) Getty/TIB c) Sunset/Wilmhurst P.135: Getty/Stone.
P.136: a) Hoaqui/Zefa/Taflan b) Bios/Decorde Bios/Delfino c) Sunset/Cournut P.137: Bios/Leduc. P.138: a) Jacana/Willemeit b) Sunset/NHPA c) Bios/Ruoso
P.139:Getty/Stone P.140: Bios/Ruoso, Sunset/Weststock P.141: up) 1) Hoaqui/PBY 2) Hoaqui/Zefa 3) Hoaqui/PBY, Sunset/Japack, Hoaqui/PBY, Getty/Stone
P.142: α & b) Getty/Taxi c) Getty/Image Bank P.143: Getty/Taxi P.144: a) Getty/Image Bank b) Bios/Delobelle c) Jacana/Bachmann P.145: Sunset/Weststock
P.146: a) Getty/Image Bank b) Getty/Taxi/Ambrose c) Jacana/Wild P.147: Getty/Taxi. P.148: a) Sunset/Diagentur b) Getty/Image Bank c) Jacana/Ziesler P.149: Getty/Stone
P.150: Jacana/Wild, Hoaqui/Galaxy/Contact, Jacana/Retherford P.151: Hoaqui/PBY, Hoaqui/Martel, Getty/Image Bank.

Chapter Land:

P.156: Sunset/Mountain Stock, Getty/Rynio, Jacana/Danegger P.157: Sunset/Horizon, Vision, Bios/Bringard, Sunset/Philips P.158: a) Bios/Klein-Hubert b) Getty/Image Bank
c) Sunset/Brunet P.159: Hoaqui/Boisvieux P.160: a) Getty/Austin b) Getty/Stone/Lewis c) Getty/Sacks P.161: Getty/Barraud P.162: a) Sunset/Spectrum b) Bios/Bringard
c) Sunset/Schang P.163: Getty/Image Bank/Close P.164: a) Sunset/NHPA b) Bios/Laboureur c) Sunset/Horizon vision P.165: Getty/Grandadam P.166: Getty/Rynio Hoaqui/Bughet
P.167: Getty/Sneesby/Wilkins, Getty/Eastrep, Bios/Bayle, Bios/Pasco P.168: a) Bios/Le Moigne b) Sunset/Christof c) Bringard/Bios P.169: Bios/Prevot P.170: a) Getty/Graham
b) Bios/Gunther c) Sunset/Ant P.171: Sunset/Animals Animals P.172: a) Getty/Veiga b) Sunset/Delfino c) Getty/Giustina P.173: Jacana/Ferguson P.174: a) Getty/Surowiak
b) Sunset/F.Stock c) Hoaqui/Hagenmüller P.175: Getty/Giustina P.176: a) Sunset/Brossard b) Hoaqui/Zefa c) Getty/Chalfant P.177: Sunset/Claudie P.178: Getty/Giustina
Hoaqui/Weisbecker P.179: Getty/Image Bank/Rossi Explorer/Geopress, Sunset/NHPA, Getty/Adams, P.180: a) Bios/Gunther b) Getty/Lepp c) Bios/Harvey P.181: Hoaqui/Lobo
P.182: a) Sunset/Weststock b) Getty/Bumgarner c) Getty/McQueen P.183: Sunset F.Stock P. 184: a) Getty/Dykinga b) Getty/Stablyck c) Hoaqui/Bughet P.185 : Sunset/Philips
P.186 : Sunset/Bercand, Getty/Mc Intire P.187 : Getty/Meola, Getty/Bean, Sunset/Mc Donald, Getty/Dole

Index: Bios/Martin, Bios/Von, Schmieder, Bios/Gunther, Bios/Klein-Hubert, Phone/Goetgheluck, Sunset/Lacz, Bios/Tavernier, Bios/publiphoto/Schell, Bios/Rotman, Sunset/FLPA

The following people have collaborated in the making of this book:
Sylvie Basdevant-Suzuki , Jim Breheny, Nathalie Cagnat, April Dahlberg, Eric Elzière, Audrey Fallope, François Guion